Printed and Bound in Belgium.

ISBN 0-517-69121-3

hgfedcba

Tales of Oaktree Wood

MANDY'S UMBRELLA

by Rene Cloke

DERRYDALE BOOKS

New York

Mandy, the woodmouse, picked up the letter
that had just arrived in the mail.

It was big and white and looked
very exciting.

"I will get my breakfast ready first,"
she decided and propped the letter
against the butter dish.

Then she sat down
at the breakfast table
and opened the envelope.

"Dear Mandy," she read,
"A few friends are coming
to lunch with me on Friday;
I shall be so pleased if
you are able to join us.

      With love, Meg."

Mandy was delighted.
"I will wear my new dress and hat; I do hope
it will be a sunny day."

But Friday was not a bright day.

It was raining and the wind was blowing
through the trees.

Mandy put on her new dress and her new hat;
she looked very pretty as she started off
through the woods with her big umbrella.

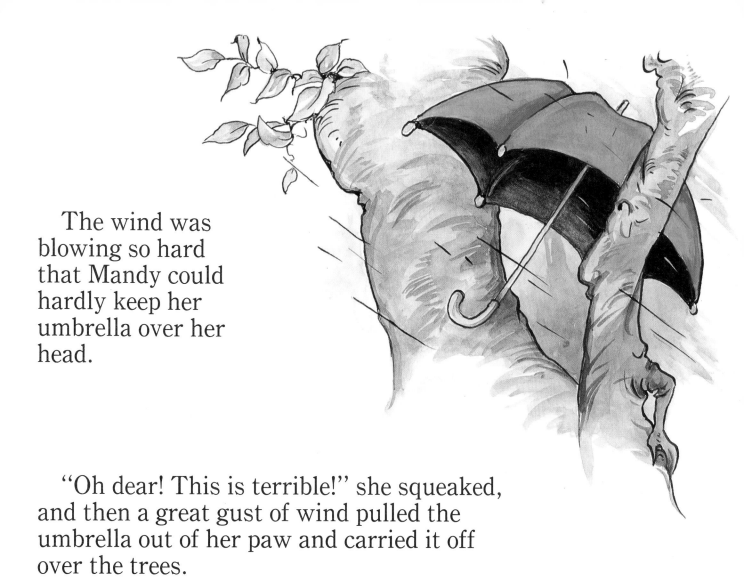

The wind was blowing so hard that Mandy could hardly keep her umbrella over her head.

"Oh dear! This is terrible!" she squeaked, and then a great gust of wind pulled the umbrella out of her paw and carried it off over the trees.

"How shall I keep dry?" moaned poor Mandy. "My pretty new hat will be ruined."

And then she saw a large mushroom. "That will do beautifully!" she cried picking up the mushroom and, holding it over her head, she hurried along.

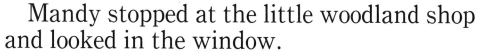

Mandy stopped at the little woodland shop
and looked in the window.
"I will buy some candy for Meg,"
she decided and, leaving
her mushroom umbrella on the porch,
she went into the shop.

As usual the shop was full of customers.
Belinda Bunny sold everything that anyone could want, and she was very busy behind the counter.
Mr. Spindle was buying a bucket and duster and Mrs. Moley wanted some apples.
The young squirrels were choosing bars of chocolate and packets of cookies and Mrs. Dora Quack-duck was asking for a loaf of bread and some butter.

It was quite a long time before Mandy
could get served. She chose a box of
mixed chocolates for her friend and Belinda
wrapped it in pretty paper.

When Mandy walked out of the shop with her package she looked around for her mushroom umbrella – it had disappeared!

Perhaps it had blown away
like her real umbrella.
"Oh well," she said,
"it has stopped raining,
so I will hurry along
as quickly as I can.
Meg's house isn't too far."

When she arrived at the little house in the
hollow tree she was greeted by all her friends,
Flippy Frog, Filbert and Sally Squirrel,
Woody Field-mouse and Noddy Dormouse.

"Come in!" cried Meg. "I am just going to make omelettes for lunch."

Everyone sat down at the table and
Meg brought in a big dish of omelettes.
   "I was very lucky," she told them,
"as I passed the shop this morning,
I saw a big mushroom outside,
so I cut it up and put it
in the omelettes."

"Why, that was my umbrella," cried Mandy, "and we are eating it!"

Everyone laughed and Mandy told them about her real umbrella blowing away.

"I know where it is," said Flippy, "it flew past me this morning and was caught in a tree near my house."

So, after lunch, all the animals went to look for the lost umbrella.

There it was,
high in the branches
of a tree.
"It's a long way up,"
said Mandy, "I wonder
if I can climb
up there."

"I'll get it for you," said Filbert and he scurried up the tree.

Since he was a very good climber, he was soon able to rescue the umbrella and give it back to Mandy.

The animals waved goodbye to Mandy
as she hurried home.
   "A good end to your adventures," they cried,
"don't lose your umbrella again,
and don't let anyone eat it!"
   But Mandy's adventures were not over.

When she reached her house, she found that the rain had left a deep pool all around the tree, right up to the doorstep.

It looked deep
and very cold.

"I don't want to get wet swimming across that,"
she said anxiously. "Now what shall I do?
I wish I had a little boat and then I could row
across to my house."
Then she had a bright idea.

She opened her umbrella and
rested it on the water.
Then she stepped gently inside and,
taking a little stick,
she pushed off
from the bank.
The umbrella was like
a real little boat.

It was a rocky ride and once the umbrella
was caught in a tuft of grass.

At last, she made her way across the pond
and reached her house.

There was some water in her umbrella but Mandy
tipped it back into the pond before she
opened the door.

"There," she said as she crept up the step
and through the door, "safely home again
and my umbrella has been very useful after all."

She hung it up on a peg and took off her
hat and coat.

"Oh, dear! I am quite tired."

She made herself a cup of tea,
put some little cakes on a tray and
went up to her bedroom to eat her snack.
  Very soon she was fast asleep and dreaming about
sailing across a huge pond in a little boat
that kept changing into an umbrella
and then into a big mushroom.

Mandy was quite glad to wake up and find her umbrella still hanging on the peg.

"Next time it rains," she said, "I will tie it to my paw."